Acting Edition

Confederates

by Dominique Morisseau

ıl SAMUEL FRENCH lı

No one shall make any changes in this title(s) for the purpose of production. No part of this book may be reproduced, stored in a retrieval system, scanned, uploaded, or transmitted in any form, by any means, now known or yet to be invented, including mechanical, electronic, digital, photocopying, recording, videotaping, or otherwise, without the prior written permission of the publisher. No one shall share this title(s), or any part of this title(s), through any social media or file hosting websites.

For all inquiries regarding motion picture, television, online/digital and other media rights, please contact Concord Theatricals Corp.

MUSIC AND THIRD-PARTY MATERIALS USE NOTE

Licensees are solely responsible for obtaining formal written permission from copyright owners to use copyrighted music and/or other copyrighted third-party materials (e.g., artworks, logos) in the performance of this play and are strongly cautioned to do so. If no such permission is obtained by the licensee, then the licensee must use only original music and materials that the licensee owns and controls. Licensees are solely responsible and liable for clearances of all third-party copyrighted materials, including without limitation music, and shall indemnify the copyright owners of the play(s) and their licensing agent, Concord Theatricals Corp., against any costs, expenses, losses and liabilities arising from the use of such copyrighted third-party materials by licensees. For music, please contact the appropriate music licensing authority in your territory for the rights to any incidental music.

IMPORTANT BILLING AND CREDIT REQUIREMENTS

If you have obtained performance rights to this title, please refer to your licensing agreement for important billing and credit requirements.

CONFEDERATES premiered at Signature Theatre in New York City on March 8, 2022. The production was directed by Stori Ayers, with scenic design by Rachel Hauck, costume design by Ari Fulton, lighting design by Amith Chandrashaker and Emma Deane, projection design by Katherine Freer, and sound design by Curtis Craig and Jimmy Keys. The production stage manager was Jonathan Castanien. The cast was as follows:

SANDRA . . . . Michelle Wilson

SARA . . . . Kristolyn Lloyd

ABNER / MALIK . . . . Elijah Jones

MISSY SUE / CANDICE . . . . Kenzie Ross

LUANNE / JADE . . . . Andrea Patterson

CHARACTERS

SANDRA – Black woman, late thirties/early forties. Scholar, professor of political science, practical, sturdy, compassionate with students, protected with her own emotions, and a striving spirit in the face of institutional racism.

SARA – Black woman, early twenties. Tenacious, spunky, tough, and resilient. A slave woman with a fighting spirit, unwilling to be broken by her circumstances. Crafty and a sharp, witty tongue. Slowly becoming a Union spy.

ABNER – Black man, early twenties. Energetic and driven. A bit stubborn but strong-willed. A runaway slave and soldier for the Union. Brother of Sara. Loves his sister fiercely. (Doubled with Malik.)

MALIK – Black man, early twenties. Studious and focused on his education. Driven and intellectually stimulating. A student of Sandra's who tries to carefully navigate her status over his. (Doubled with Abner.)

MISSY SUE – White woman, late twenties/early thirties. Spirited, driven, a strong sense of duty and mission. Somewhat oblivious. Emotionally free and open. Daughter of Sara's Master. Sara's former childhood friend. (Doubled with Candice.)

CANDICE – White woman, mid-twenties. Loquacious, intellectually curious, and uncensored in her ideas. Can be misinterpreted as insensitive but is likely unaware. Emotionally free and open. Student and assistant to Sandra. (Doubled with Missy Sue.)

LUANNE – Black woman, early twenties. Curious, eager, and inquisitive. A fellow slave with Sara, who has been afforded privileges Sara has not. In an affair with the Master. Pushing for kinship with Sara. (Doubled with Jade.)

JADE – Black woman, late thirties/early forties. Straight shooter, unafraid of confrontation, down-to-earth. Fellow professor and colleague to Sandra. Navigates institutional racism more directly than Sandra. (Doubled with LuAnne.)

AUTHOR'S NOTE

This play is not like all of my others. If you are familiar with my work, you may know me to sit in naturalistic drama, with some humor. You may be used to earnest social dramas with a political backdrop. This play, while still derived from my same heart and compassion, is not as earnest as the others. There are hills and valleys in this play, places where it lives on the ground in naturalism, and lots of other places where naturalism betrays you and we are straight up in satire. The bigger you are willing to go, both in the world of slavery and in the present, the more earned and powerful the moments will be that hit on the ground. But without going big, without being loud and a lil' crazy and unhinged in places...without, for instance, going straight up "Gone With the Wind" in the Missy Sue scenes, the play will not work. If you don't think this play is funny, you are missing a lot of my play.

In fact, this play hits every humorous funny bone, in the past especially, but also in the present. In Scenes 8 and 9, we are going into straight up farce. I dub these two scenes "the circus." Because this is when all of the characters come together, and there are people entering the scenes before other people have fully left. There is hide-and-go-seek and "who's on first" behavior going on. To serve my play is to find a great deal of levity in the absurdity of the worlds. And to also trust and allow the real and deep moments to hit the bottom of the ocean. You'll know where these are if you trust the gravity of the story. (Hint: they are usually close to the monologues.)

There are reasons for this chosen style. Sometimes existing in the middle of racism, sexism, classism, and the insanity of it all is like living through a farce. Sometimes the enslaved HAD to be thinking, "No this bitch didn't just say..." just like we think about things now! Let the past and the present merge in consciousness. Let there be overlaps. The point is, it will be hard to tell the worlds apart because the shit is just being recycled over and over again.

May you have fun during the mounting of this play. If you are not having fun, you're taking the play too seriously. And missing the weight of what is to come. By the end of the play, we are stealing everyone's breath. And the only way to get them open enough to achieve this is to find and explore the humor along with the pain.

I trust you to find the laughter, the profundity, the rage, and the heart. Let's make art and get free...

peaceandlovedominique:)

1.

(Lights rise on a woman, **SANDRA**. *She is dressed in a power suit. She takes a sip of water. Pushes a button on a remote, and a slide is shown. Image of a Black woman slave with a white baby suckling her bare breast.* **SANDRA** *clicks off the image.)*

SANDRA. Before this becomes a complete misinterpretation of intent, I'd like to say that I am not averse to images of slavery. They do not embarrass or fatigue me. I supported *Roots*. Watched all seven volumes. My mother made me. I think I was nine. Her idea of summer vacation. I read *Jubilee*. The freedom papers of Frederick Douglass. The slave narratives of Olaudah Equiano, Mary Prince and Harriet Jacobs. I have seen *12 Years a Slave, Slave Play, The Slave,* another play – not the same, *Birth of a Nation, The Birth of a Nation* – very different movies, *Father Comes Home from the Wars, An Octoroon, Harriet, Underground, Underground Railroad, Amistad, Sankofa, Beloved, Unchained Memories, Uncle Tom's Cabin, Glory,* and even *Django Unchained,* though there are serious debates to be had over the qualifications of that last one. I have visited the International Slavery Museum in Liverpool, the Slavery Human Zoo in Moscow – yes, you heard that right, they had a human zoo, the Middle Passage Exhibit at the Charles H. Wright Museum of African American History in Detroit – some children on a field trip threw up on a model of the slave ship – understandably – it's a very convincing diorama, the National Underground Railroad Freedom Center in Cincinnati – an elderly man with dementia, no doubt, mistook our tour guide for Harriet Tubman. I've visited the African Burial Grounds in Manhattan, the Slave Mart Museum in Charleston, the National Museum of African American History and Culture in DC, and walked the shores of Ghana where the slave castles are still standing. I even discuss the impact of slavery in my Comparative Politics Classes. There is nothing slavery that is off limits for me. No shame in my own enslaved heritage. NO SHAME. And yet...

> *(She presses the remote. The slide shifts. Becomes even larger and more grotesque. The woman slave now has Sandra's face, Photoshopped onto the original.* **SANDRA** *takes a breath.)*

It was hanging on my office door. After office hours. Sometime between five p.m. yesterday and nine a.m. this morning. I'm not sure what...it is trying to say... but I demand an investigation. It is imperative that the student who placed this upon my door be put on academic probation immediately. Thank you for giving me the floor.

2.

(Lights up in a slave cabin. A bed and a fireplace with a pot on it, brewing. Where are we? Have we time-traveled?)

*(A man, **ABNER**, lies on the bed as a woman, **SARA**, sews up his wound with a needle and thread.)*

ABNER. Ow, gotdamn Sara!

SARA. Be calm and lemme work. Can't stop the needle from pokin' if my subject keep floppin' around like a dead fish.

ABNER. Said you knew what you was doin'.

SARA. Do.

ABNER. Said you sewed up two blacksmiths and four runaways.

SARA. Did.

ABNER. Then why it feel like you don't know the difference between my ribs and my ass?

SARA. Dark.

ABNER. Pull me closer to the fire if you can't see. I ain't gon' keep gettin' poked in the wrong places.

SARA. You the nurse now?

ABNER. I'm the soldier.

SARA. Shut it! You want somebody to hear you sayin' that loud?

ABNER. Let 'em. I'm proud.

SARA. Gon' be proud and dead.

*(She sticks the needle into his abdomen and stitches. **ABNER** hisses from pain.)*

SARA. Need to bite a pillow? I got a satchel of feathers over there.

ABNER. I'm fine. I'm a man. I'm a soldier. I'm fine.

SARA. Stop calling yourself that. Be proud and quiet. Last thing we need is for LuAnne to hear you talking. She the fastest snitch on the whole plantation. Master Dan got her wrapped around his finger. More loyal to him than she is to her own god.

ABNER. Let her be that. She got her own way to make due. You don't wanna be none of that.

SARA. I know I don't.

ABNER. You good 'n' safe with what you do right now. Fast picker. Keep out of the eye of the storm. You like the nighttime nobody seem to notice. That's good 'n' safe. I ain't got to worry as much.

SARA. Don't wanna be safe. Wanna be useful.

ABNER. I told you no.

SARA. Why not?

ABNER. Ain't for womanfolk.

SARA. Cuz you braver? That's what you think?

ABNER. Ain't gon' fuss about this with you no mo'.

SARA. I been sewed up 'bout five times before. Once from getting sliced with a piece of sharp wood from Missy Sue cuz I could read better 'n' her so she stopped learnin' me. Once from a glass Mistress threw at my head for askin' if I could sleep inside the house with Missy Sue since we was friends and such. And three other times from fights out here in the field and I ain't never screamed or hissed like you been doin' ever since I threaded this needle. How you figurin' this ain't for womanfolk? It ain't not-for-womanfolk neither.

ABNER. I told you we ain't fussin' and I mean it! And you gon' stop sayin' you can read like it's just everyday okay.

Ain't a faster way for a gal to get lynched then to be actin' smart.

SARA. You stop sayin' you a soldier all loud and proud, I'll stop sayin' I can read.

> (**ABNER** *sighs loudly with exhaustion.* **SARA** *truly and really exhausts him.*)
>
> (**SARA** *sews quietly.*)

ABNER. We movin' down westward. Two days mo' and we'll be crossing the state lines.

SARA. And then I won't be seein' you?

ABNER. When it's over, you'll see me anytime you want.

SARA. You the only brother I got left.

ABNER. And you gon' see me. I'll come back for you.

SARA. I should come with you. You gon' need a nurse.

ABNER. Not the way you stitching.

SARA. I mean it.

ABNER. No Sara. The mens would have their way with you. You get caught and I wouldn't be able to protect you. You safer here.

SARA. Safer. Here???

ABNER. This, you already know. This, you got skill in. Hands know how to pull to keep from gettin' whipped. Know how to birth them chir'ren for all the womens so they don't get sick and die 'fore the babies come out. You barren as the forest in the winter. Nobody come messin' with you. Everybody know you got the *mark*, but them skills make you useful. Out there in the trenches? Got to get learned all over again. Ain't safe.

SARA. You ain't no safer. Runaway turned Union soldier. They find you they chop your head off and eat it for supper.

ABNER. 'Least I'll die like a man.

SARA. How I'm gon' die?

ABNER. Free. That's why I'm fightin'.

SARA. I want to die like a man too.

>   (*ABNER sighs again.*)

ABNER. You make less and less sense the mo' you talk.

SARA. Then stop talking to me.

>   (*She finishes the last stitch. Pats his side.*)

Done.

>   (*ABNER stands up slowly.*)

ABNER. You a good nurse.

SARA. Ain't the way to flatter me.

ABNER. You a good sister.

SARA. I want to come with you.

ABNER. I won't have it.

SARA. I can fight. Hold me one of them muskets and see what I could do.

>   (*She eyes his musket nearby. Picks it up. He hastens over to her as best he can through his pain.*)

ABNER. Damnit, I told you don't touch it!

SARA. Just want to see how it feels. Real mighty. Like I could gather me a bunch of kinfolk and walk right off the plantation.

ABNER. You gon' hurt yourself.

SARA. You hurt yourself. Only soldier to fall on his own sword.

ABNER. Got stabbed. Told you that. With a knife.

SARA. Yo' own knife. In practice, not combat.

ABNER. Was gettin' ready for combat.

SARA. I can do it Abner. I can be a good soldier. I can free 'em from every plantation. You could show me how to use it. I'd be good.

ABNER. Sara –

SARA. 'Least let me hold it. Show me how. So I know what it feels like to have the power of freedom in my hands. 'Case I never see you again.

> (**ABNER** *looks at his sister. He loves her. She is exhausting, but she is fierce.*)
>
> (*He picks up the musket. Walks over to her slowly Takes her hand and places it on the weapon. Aims it out for her.*)

ABNER. (*As if he is knighting her with an honor.*) Now you're a real man.

> (*Lights shift.* **ABNER** *steps out of the scene and moves into the next as if he is stepping into a new time period...with a new name... and a new identity.*)

3.

(Lights up on **SANDRA** *in her office. Sitting atop her desk. The actor who just played* **ABNER** *is now a student,* **MALIK.** *He sits across from* **SANDRA,** *a laptop in his hands. He looks at it with perplexity.)*

MALIK. Un-thorough and incomplete in its analysis.

SANDRA. Is that what I wrote?

MALIK. It is.

SANDRA. Then I stand by it.

MALIK. I pulled two all-nighters.

SANDRA. You should get better rest, Malik.

MALIK. I drank six cups of coffee. Four Red Bulls. My eyes were bleeding from fatigue, but I delivered all twenty pages. Proofread. Well-structured. Footnotes. A bibliography. And citations. I don't understand.

SANDRA. I gave you a B-.

MALIK. That pulls my whole average down. I'm on scholarship. I need an A.

SANDRA. I've given you the option like I give to all of my students to re-do the paper if you want a higher grade. I'll take the balance between the two. You know this Malik.

MALIK. Professor, it's a political science essay. There has to be room for opinion, is that not correct?

SANDRA. That is correct. Opinion based on thorough research and in-depth analysis. This is Comparative Politics, Malik.

MALIK. Lincoln didn't sign the Emancipation Proclamation out of some bleeding heart desire to end the institution of slavery. Many of my resources back up that claim.

SANDRA. I'm not denying that claim. I'm saying there are loopholes in your overall analysis of the so-called modern-day plantation in the workforce and its parallel to slavery during the time of the Civil War.

MALIK. My uncle works on Wall Street. He backed up my analysis as very plausible and effective.

SANDRA. Your uncle didn't write your paper.

MALIK. I'm not saying that. I'm saying the way Black workers in corporate America are treated, the divide that happens among them, the way in which they operate in silos, are often overlooked for promotion, are not operating within equal access to advancement opportunities, are policed for their cultural grooming and attire, and are overall suffocated and denied access to the controlled systems of wealth, this is some modern-day peculiar institution-type shit.

SANDRA. Malik –

MALIK. Excuse me, Professor. Stuff. Not shit.

SANDRA. Okay, I read everything you just recapped. My questions, which you have yet to consider, lie in your failure to distinguish the variables in policy. What is the equivalent to the Emancipation Proclamation in your analysis? Affirmative action?

MALIK. That's correct.

SANDRA. But you fail to draw an effective parallel.

MALIK. Affirmative action, a policy which was put into executive order by JFK, was intended to ensure that applicants are employed without discrimination to race, gender, what have you. Emancipation Proclamation, put into executive order by Lincoln, was intended to abolish the act of slavery, which was being systemized through the free labor of Africans in America.

SANDRA. You're only re-stating the essay. I remember this statement. Move forward.

MALIK. Neither of these policies originally targeted the people it was designed to protect. They both came with multiple side clauses and loopholes. The result, slaves still weren't freed even after the proclamation, and so-called minorities weren't employed equally after affirmative action. Paperwork and lies and bullshit and plantation by another name.

SANDRA. Okay, Malik.

MALIK. Bull-stuff.

SANDRA. I admire your passion. I think you can draw more concise lines between corporate America and the plantation. It's not absurd. It's just...not an easy route to follow. I admire your passion though, I really do.

MALIK. Please don't patronize me, Professor.

SANDRA. I'm not patronizing.

MALIK. You admire my passion? That's not patronizing?

SANDRA. I realize you have some disagreements with my curriculum.

MALIK. That's not what this is about.

SANDRA. You've made it clear several times that you think I'm not giving enough balanced framework in my lessons on unconscious bias.

MALIK. Am I not able to challenge?

SANDRA. No, you're able. That's what this class is for.

MALIK. Then why the hard time, Professor?

SANDRA. Hard time? What hard time?

MALIK. I just feel like you...don't respect me much.

SANDRA. Why would I not respect you? I respect all of my students.

MALIK. I try really hard.

SANDRA. I recognize that. I encourage the effort and am pushing for you to go further.

MALIK. I don't think you acknowledge the effort I make. I think you only push but don't ever affirm.

SANDRA. Really?

MALIK. Yes really.

SANDRA. Wow.

> (**SANDRA** *takes a moment to process this. It catches her off-guard.*)

MALIK. Is it because I'm a man?

SANDRA. WHAT?

MALIK. I'm asking a sincere – not trying to disrespect –

SANDRA. Why would you – whhh – what are you implying?

MALIK. Nothing. Nevermind.

SANDRA. No, what are you – what in the hell –

MALIK. I feel bias. Sometimes.

SANDRA. From???

MALIK. You. Toward other women in the class. Away from me.

SANDRA. How so?

MALIK. Like the other day.

SANDRA. What other day?

MALIK. You wore a particular shirt to class.

SANDRA. Black Lives Matter.

MALIK. Yes, that particular shirt.

SANDRA. I'm not following. Did you...take offense –

MALIK. No.

SANDRA. Okay, because I'd be surprised –

MALIK. It's just what you emphasized about the shirt.

SANDRA. I'm sorry?

MALIK. Of who started that particular movement.

SANDRA. You mean the women.

MALIK. Yes.

SANDRA. Three women.

MALIK. Yes, I know. And that's cool. But your emphasis...

SANDRA. My emphasis?

MALIK. Made it seem as if that was the most important fact about the movement. That it was started...that it was those three women. And not –

SANDRA. I know why it was started. We all know why it was started.

MALIK. I feel a personal connection to why it was started.

SANDRA. Understandably.

MALIK. But the way you emphasized...the way you sometimes emphasize things in class... I just feel that there is a bias. Unconscious. That you may carry –

SANDRA. I don't do that.

MALIK. Okay.

SANDRA. Malik.

MALIK. Yes?

SANDRA. I don't do that.

MALIK. Okay.

SANDRA. Okay.

> (*Pause.* **SANDRA** *sips some water.* **MALIK** *types furiously on his laptop.*)

What's that, are you –

MALIK. Taking notes.

> (**SANDRA** *nods. Concerned. Tries to regroup. Start over.*)

SANDRA. Okay, Malik. I think this is truth time. Okay?

MALIK. Okay.

SANDRA. I think you're one of the brightest students in my class.

MALIK. Okay.

SANDRA. And I think... I think your mind is sharp and focused. This is genuine. Not patronizing.

MALIK. Okay.

SANDRA. I've worked here for seven years. I'm tenured. I've seen lots of minds. You're one of those unforgettable ones.

MALIK. You've never told me that.

SANDRA. Sometimes you tell a student. Sometimes you just observe and push. I see now that I needed to balance my strategy with you. But I have to push. For a number of reasons, I have to push you. I have to make sure your work is airtight. Do you understand?

MALIK. Because I'm a Black man.

SANDRA. Because there will be many doubts about you here. About whether or not you're equipped. Deserving of the scholarship. And I won't allow it to take up space.

MALIK. I think I understand.

SANDRA. You know, my father was a political science major and a mathematical genius? Math and global liberation were linked, he'd say. It's the only universal language. If you can teach people to solve for x around the world, they can solve hunger and injustice too. This went on well into my teens, until one day my father had a stroke and suffered brain damage. He was permanently paralyzed on the left side of his body, but his mind was still sharp.

He always believed that one day, he could solve for x and learn to walk again. He never stopped believing that...

(**SANDRA** *is swept away in her own truth.* **MALIK** *notices.*)

MALIK. Professor? You alright?

SANDRA. I lost my father earlier this year. He never did walk again.

MALIK. Oh. I'm so sorry.

(**SANDRA** *returns to herself. To the present world.*)

SANDRA. My point is. He refused to be defeated by disability. And you remind me so much of my father, Malik. As long as your mind is sharp, no one can limit you. You will always be undefeatable. Do you understand?

MALIK. Yes.

SANDRA. You do?

MALIK. Yes, I think so.

SANDRA. Good.

(*A moment.*)

MALIK. And this is why even though my paper is solid, even though I never miss a day of class or am even a second late, even though I have footnotes and a bibliography and citations, that you still give my paper a B-. Because you want me to be limitless. Is that correct?

(*Pause.* **SANDRA** *eyes* **MALIK.** *His tone is curious.*)

SANDRA. Malik –

MALIK. Because, Professor, I know what bias I face when I walk into the room. What assumptions will be made. The accusations of me being unfit for my scholarship. I know what fear I put into the heart of my classmates when I disagree with them. The ways in which I have to make myself small so they don't think I'm angry. The ways that I have to make myself agreeable in order to seem grateful enough to be given free money for my education. The way my white classmates on the same scholarship have the comfort of feeling entitled while I have the discomfort of feeling, like, un-entitled. And when I get a Black professor, she tells me that I should work harder and be smarter so that I can have a fair chance. My Black professor, who has the ability to give me a fair chance, but because she feels the need to prove her tenure worthiness to her colleagues, won't give me the fair chance. Wants me to exceed a bias that I didn't have a hand in creating. Yes, Professor, I think I get it all now. Thank you.

(SANDRA *eyes* MALIK *again.*)

SANDRA. You can turn the paper back in to me in the morning. By nine a.m. With a more in-depth analysis and clearer points that aren't mired down by footnotes and quotes by other writers. Your own words. Your own ideas. Not your uncle's. Yours. Tomorrow. That is all I have left to say.

(MALIK *types something furiously on his laptop again. Then closes it and gets up.*)

MALIK. Cool.

SANDRA. And as for the comment about gender bias –

MALIK. Yes?

SANDRA. Affirmative action was also being used to create opportunities for gender-employment equity. That means it was seriously lacking. Some scholars argue that it was even more about gender equity than racial.

MALIK. Obviously.

SANDRA. I'm sorry, obviously?

MALIK. Your presence here.

SANDRA. Excuse me?

MALIK. Of my twelve professors here, six are white men. Four are white women. And then there's you and Professor Banks. No Black male professors anywhere.

SANDRA. I'm sorry, is this going somewhere I should be aware of?

MALIK. Perhaps things would be different on my paper if there were more balance in professors.

SANDRA. You think as a Black woman professor I have it easier than Black men? Is that your implication?

MALIK. The demographic of my professors is a fact. That's all I can say.

SANDRA. You have. No. Idea.

MALIK. Tomorrow morning. I'll have a new paper. I'll try again. I always try. That's all I know to do.

(*He heads to the door.*)

Also I'm really sorry about that picture that was put on your door. That's fucked up. For real.

(**MALIK** *walks out.* **SANDRA** *is left...disturbed...*)

4.

(SARA reads the Bible by candlelight in her cabin.)

SARA. *(Aloud to herself.)* When you are approaching the battle, the priest shall come near and speak to the people. He shall say to them...

(She sets down the book. Picks up a stick and aims it as a rifle. Recites the Bible from memory.)

Hear, O Israel, you are approaching the battle against your enemies today. Do not be afraid, or panic, or tremble before them, for the LORD your God is the one who goes with you, to fight for you against your enemies.

(A knock comes to her cabin door. SARA jumps and quickly shoves the book inside a satchel of feathers and tries to attempt normal. She walks to the door.)

Who's it?

MISSY SUE. *(Offstage.)* It's me! Missy Sue! Open up Sara.

(SARA is thoroughly perplexed. What in the hell? She opens the door cautiously.)

SARA. Missy who?

(MISSY SUE enters and grabs SARA in an embrace.)

MISSY SUE. It's me Sara. My god, it's been ages!

SARA. Missy Sue? What you doin' down here at night?

MISSY SUE. I came to pay a visit to my long-lost friend.

SARA. That's me?

MISSY SUE. Of course it's you! Why wouldn't it be you?

SARA. Um...

MISSY SUE. Look at you Sara. Your skin is still so perfect. Your frame so healthy. You've aged well.

SARA. I suppose. Good as possible for being a slave and all.

MISSY SUE. You are still sassy. That clever sass. I miss it so much.

SARA. You s'pose to have went north, ain't it? To live with your new husband and bear you some chir'ren. Never thought I'd see you again.

MISSY SUE. Oh it didn't happen that way, Sara. Nothing happens the way they tell you. Much as we tried I just couldn't bear him any children. It was awful. I nearly died inside. What's a woman without bearing fruit and multiplying? There isn't a place for us, Sara.

SARA. I know it. I'm barren as winter.

MISSY SUE. It can suffocate you, Sara. Make you lose purpose. Vision.

SARA. I just said I know it too.

MISSY SUE. But then there's a light somewhere. Something that tells you you'll either die or find something worth fighting and dying *for*.

SARA. I know that too. Got my something real clear.

MISSY SUE. Me too, Sara. That's why I'm here. You remember how close we were as friends. You remember all I taught you?

SARA. I remember a lot of things.

MISSY SUE. You remember us reading the Bible together?

SARA. I do.

MISSY SUE. I taught you wrong, you know that?

SARA. The Bible? Wrong?

MISSY SUE. I taught you the passage of Titus, chapter two verse nine:

Bid slaves to be submissive to their masters and to give satisfaction in every respect; they are not to be refractory, nor to pilfer, but to show entire and true fidelity. Do you remember that?

SARA. I do. You used to make me repeat it to you.

MISSY SUE. That was wrong of me. Completely wrong.

SARA. Was it now?

MISSY SUE. I met some friends upon my travels, Sara. Some very important friends. Oh my god, there is so much to tell you. Let me sit down. Take a breath. Take you in.

SARA. Got the one wood chair. I guess you gon' take that so...take it.

(**MISSY SUE** *walks over and takes the chair.*)

MISSY SUE. Papa is getting good and fat, Sara. Have you noticed?

(**SARA** *looks at* **MISSY SUE** *sideways. Knows good and damn well she can't answer that question.*)

SARA. That something *you* noticed?

MISSY SUE. Eating everything on his plate, and everyone else's too.

SARA. Can't imagine how it'd all fit.

MISSY SUE. It's bottomless, his appetite. I think it always has been. Insatiable.

SARA. Hm.

MISSY SUE. I never felt a connection, you know. To him. Or Mother. Or anyone. I always felt that I belonged among the people who knew me best. People like you and my other good girl, Lula. And of course that was impossible. But now that Mother's passed from the yellow fever, it's just me and Father. And since Robert ran off –

SARA. Robert, your husband?

MISSY SUE. That's right Sara. You never met him but that was his name. Robert. Lousy in finance and lousy in the bedroom. Lousy in every way they come. Except, of course, he exposed me to opportunities, so I suppose I should be grateful for that.

SARA. You like it up north?

MISSY SUE. In many ways yes, but don't let Papa hear me saying that. He never liked Robert much and thinks the north finished up and ruined me. Doesn't like to hear my ideas for social progression. I attended very promising meetings in the north, Sara. It's all I could do when Robert was out philandering. I filled my calendar with meetings and clubs and conversations among social progressives.

SARA. Sounds busier than picking cotton.

(**MISSY SUE** *laughs.*)

MISSY SUE. That's funny, Sara. You are really funny. Of course it isn't. I wouldn't ever imply such a thing. Picking cotton that one time when the hurricane threatened to take all of our crops and we all had to lay hand to the field...that was hell on me. I was only twelve years old. I don't know how you've been doing it since the age of seven. I really don't know.

SARA. Strong hands.

(**MISSY SUE** *looks at* **SARA.** *Was that a dig? She decides to quickly forgive it.*)

MISSY SUE. Right. Naturally. Of course. Listen, Sara, I always believed you to be very smart. I've taught many students, but never one with a mind like yours. You speak so well. Do you still take to the reading?

SARA. It's illegal, Missy Sue. It wouldn't make sense for me to do that.

(MISSY SUE *eyes* SARA *curiously.*)

MISSY SUE. Right. Of course.

SARA. Everything you taught me, I already forgot it.

MISSY SUE. Sara, you don't have to –

SARA. Brain empty as that sack of feathers.

(MISSY SUE *eyes the sack of feathers.*)

MISSY SUE. You mean this one over here?

(*She walks toward it.* SARA *remembers her Bible is stuffed inside and heads* MISSY SUE *off.* SARA *grabs the satchel and moves it away.*)

SARA. You don't wanna touch none of that, Missy Sue. Mary from the field had her baby on that very satchel. Delivered it myself. Ain't had a chance to wash it yet.

(MISSY SUE *watches* SARA.)

MISSY SUE. Oh goodness, of course.

SARA. It sure is good to see you all grown up though. Sorry about your husband running off and you being barren and your daddy not paying you any attention. Must be real hard on you. You take care of yourself now.

(SARA *opens the door.* MISSY SUE *remains still.*)

MISSY SUE. Sara.

SARA. Yes, Missy?

MISSY SUE. I'm not ready to leave yet.

SARA. No?

MISSY SUE. No.

SARA. What can I do for you? Fix you supper? They barely give me a full slice of beef and some jars of rice, but I guess you gon' take that if you wants it, so –

MISSY SUE. I want to talk to you. Privately. Woman to woman.

SARA. Woman to...woman?

MISSY SUE. I know you don't have reason to understand anything that I'm going to tell you, but I'm here to help you, Sara.

SARA. I'm doing fine out here, thank you. Being a slave has its days, but it's alright.

MISSY SUE. Sara, that's not true.

SARA. It isn't?

MISSY SUE. Being a slave is horrible.

SARA. It is?

MISSY SUE. And I can't bear to see someone I love in such horrible conditions.

SARA. Me?

MISSY SUE. Yes, Sara. You.

SARA. You love me?

MISSY SUE. I always have. I just didn't have the courage to tell you. But something about having everything stripped of you as a woman...you find your bravery.

> (**SARA** *looks at* **MISSY SUE**. *This is all strange as hell. How is she going to get out of this?*)

SARA. I would've never guessed that one, Missy Sue.

MISSY SUE. Sara, you've been a dear friend to me and I wasn't kind as a young girl. It wasn't the way I wanted to be. It was simply the circumstances, you understand? In truth, you've always been the best friend I ever had. You would listen to me. You would nurse my wounds. You would play dolls with me and read books with me and let me dream without telling me that it's silly or insignificant.

SARA. That's what I'm supposed to do. I'm a slave.

(*Sobering for* MISSY SUE.)

MISSY SUE. Right. That's a good point, Sara. Still. It meant something. It's taken up a place in my heart.

SARA. Glad to make you feel loved, Missy.

MISSY SUE. And I want you to feel loved, Sara.

SARA. I do. By my brother, Abner. By my mama Carrie Lynn 'fo the knight riders took her for trying to steal me a piece of honeydew. I known deep love before.

MISSY SUE. I want you to feel the ultimate love, Sara.

SARA. What kind of love is that?

MISSY SUE. Freedom.

> (SARA *pauses. Looks at* MISSY SUE. *These magic words come with a lot of skepticism. And allure.)*

SARA. What you –

MISSY SUE. I know Abner was here recently, Sara.

SARA. I can't speak to or verify that Missy –

MISSY SUE. You don't have to. I know it. I know because I know the men he is crossing westward with. They are Union soldiers, Sara. And they are fighting for your freedom.

SARA. Without me?

MISSY SUE. Well, Papa says they're fighting to preserve states' rights, but your freedom is coming with it, like it or not.

SARA. It is?

MISSY SUE. But only if we ensure the success of the Union.

SARA. How you gonna do that?

MISSY SUE. I'm going to do it with your help.

SARA. My help?

MISSY SUE. I'm going to get you a position inside the house. Papa has promised me. For all my woes and for feeling blue, he'll grant me whatever I desire.

SARA. And you desire for me to work in the big house?

MISSY SUE. Yes. That's it Sara. And then you and I will be able to talk in the open. And no one will suspect a thing. And you will clean Papa's office. And listen as he instructs his fellow councilmembers on the progression of the Confederacy. And you and I together will gather a list of information. And then you'll give it to your brother when he returns.

SARA. Abner is a runaway, Missy. He ain't returning 'til we free.

MISSY SUE. He'll return. It's already been addressed among the higher ranks. And you'll pass him information, Sara. That you and I gather from Papa.

SARA. I think maybe you might be a bit mistaken, Missy.

MISSY SUE. It's because you don't trust me, is that it? You think I'm just setting you up to get Abner caught and hung?

SARA. ...

    ...

    ...

MISSY SUE. Okay, I understand your doubts Sara. Truly I do. But we are women, are we not? Both barren as winter. Isn't there something inherent that you can sense in your fruitless womb? Something that tells you a pure intention of loyalty?

SARA. ...

...

...

MISSY SUE. It's late Sara. You need rest. I'll return in the morning with the order to reassign you. Think. Pray. Read the Bible in your satchel.

SARA. What / Bible?

MISSY SUE. Let the voice of God lead you to your answer. You and I, Sara, we've never belonged where we were. And now is time for both of us to step into our destinies. This is the only thing I can bear, Sara. The gift of freedom. To those who I've always loved the most.

> (**MISSY SUE** *walks over to* **SARA** *and gives her a kiss on the mouth.*)

Goodnight, Sara.

> (*And she leaves.*)

> (**SARA** *is dumbfounded.*)

5.

(Lights up on **SANDRA** *in her office. Before her, a white female student,* **CANDICE** *[the same actress who plays* **MISSY SUE***]*. **CANDICE** *places Post-it notes on Sandra's board with a scheduling planner in her hands.)*

CANDICE. The ones in pink are all of the office requests that came in today for students in your eleven o'clock. The blues are lunch requests that you haven't yet confirmed. Note this neon green one with Dean Whitfield. I thought you might want to pay special attention to that one, as his assistant has asked me to make it a priority for you.

SANDRA. Wow. That's a lot of Post-its.

CANDICE. I thought I'd try a new system. Since you completely hated the email folders I created.

SANDRA. I didn't hate them Candice. I greatly appreciated them. I just don't do well with hidden emails.

CANDICE. Or emails in general.

SANDRA. Okay, fine.

CANDICE. It's no problem, Professor. I appreciate being given this opportunity to work with you and earn extra income to put toward my room and board. This job saved my life, actually.

SANDRA. How's your financial aid coming?

CANDICE. I'll be cut off next semester because apparently my parents make too much money. Which is basically only about a thousand bucks over the required income cap. It's completely ridiculous, but whatever. I know I can't complain about anything anymore because, well, I'm white. So there's that.

SANDRA. Did someone say that to you? Or is this self-analysis?

CANDICE. It's said in subliminals. You get a feeling around campus with all the protests and rallies going on all the time that stuff is intense. No one wants to hear a middle-class girl's problems.

SANDRA. Social unrest doesn't mean you stop having personal problems. We live in a society of multiple realities.

CANDICE. Anyway, I'm aware of my white privilege so I don't have a problem with it. I know there's some stuff I'm not supposed to complain about. It's like when you want to take a twenty-minute shower but after ten minutes the dorm water just goes lukewarm and it's like, annoying as shit but I'm completely aware that kids in Flint are dying from a two-minute shower that's full of lead or like children in Taiwan have no running water whatsoever, so basically I just have to take the ten-minute shower and appreciate it for the mediocrity that it is.

SANDRA. Interesting comparisons.

CANDICE. Only sometimes after a really bad breakup with your high-school sweetheart who swore he'd stay committed to you for four years and then you'd graduate together and have six babies and suddenly he can't even last one month before calling you like – ooops, I stuck my privileged dick in two sorority girls and I don't think I can be faithful for four years so let's just cut our losses now and avoid further damage. And I'm like, how are you measuring damage because I totally fucking picked this college to be closer to him and I could've had like a way better financial package if I stayed in-state but now I'm working like a slave – no offense – to pay off my fucking tuition and still have money for food and after this nuclear bomb-level of a phone call basically blowing up what was not much of a life in the first place, a measly ten-minute shower is just really not gonna fucking cut it. But maybe that's my privilege talking.

(**SANDRA** *chooses not to respond. She busies herself with Post-it notes and sorting. Notices something of concern.*)

SANDRA. Candice, what's this note say? Malik Powers requested to speak with me again?

CANDICE. That was from last week. You missed the meeting.

SANDRA. I did?

CANDICE. You were really busy with midterms and said to just make a list of all requests for office hours and you'd deal with it after the break.

SANDRA. I didn't see this in my inbox.

CANDICE. This was during the switchover. They're still there. In the folder that says "Student Office-Hour Requests."

SANDRA. I don't see that folder.

CANDICE. It's inside the folder that says "General Scheduling" under the category "Office Calendar."

(**SANDRA** *clicks around on her computer.*)

SANDRA. It's the e-version of a clown car...

CANDICE. Your inbox was a bit of a mess, Professor. I was just trying to clean it up.

SANDRA. How many requests did I ignore?

CANDICE. About ten. But you said you'd get back to them. Your head was spinning when I first brought them to your attention.

SANDRA. Shit. That's a lot of requests.

CANDICE. It's okay. Most of us cut you slack.

SANDRA. What?

CANDICE. The class. We get it. We don't hold it against you.

SANDRA. What does that – why?

CANDICE. We know you were…you know, struggling…

SANDRA. How was I –???

CANDICE. Forget it. It's none of my business. I'm just the hired help.

SANDRA. Candice.

CANDICE. I don't want to be in your business.

SANDRA. That's quite obvious.

CANDICE. The women in class. We get it. All been through crazy breakups. I just told you about mine. There's a sisterhood to this. We let it go. Everyone has a right to be crazy when they're…

SANDRA. Getting divorced?

CANDICE. We can just call it "the thing" if that makes it easier.

SANDRA. I'm not ashamed of my divorce.

CANDICE. Of course not. That's why we respect you so much.

SANDRA. But it's not an excuse or…

CANDICE. You don't have to explain to me.

SANDRA. Candice, if I made a mistake or overlooked something in my…that's not an excuse. I don't want to be coddled. I want to be made aware of my missteps. That's why you're assisting me. Is that clear?

CANDICE. Yes, Professor. My apologies.

SANDRA. I'd like a list of all of the students who have yet to receive office hours with me. They will be my priority.

CANDICE. What about Malik Powers?

SANDRA. What about him?

CANDICE. He's already met with you twice. Other students haven't met with you at all.

SANDRA. Then that's an oversight. We need to correct it. He'll have to wait.

CANDICE. Well...not really an oversight.

SANDRA. I'm sorry?

CANDICE. I sort of told you about the other students and you seemed to only be interested in addressing Malik's concerns. Figured he wanted to deal with something pretty important.

SANDRA. I care about all of the students.

CANDICE. Right. No doubt. Wasn't suggesting –

SANDRA. So then what –

CANDICE. Nothing.

SANDRA. Okay.

(A moment.)

Candice, have students expressed concerns about my office hours?

CANDICE. I wouldn't know.

SANDRA. I think you would.

CANDICE. I don't...share it. So...

SANDRA. Share what?

CANDICE. The attitude that you seem to have bias.

SANDRA. You think I have bias?

CANDICE. Not me, no.

SANDRA. For whom? Malik?

CANDICE. Some students might think that but they're just thin-skinned. I get it. You should have some connection. You both have a bond. White kids are just jealous.

SANDRA. What – wait a – okay. That's not correct. I don't have a bias toward Malik. Everyone seems to think there's a bias toward something.

CANDICE. People respect you, Professor. They just wanna be close. You're like kind of a big deal.

SANDRA. I'm just a professor.

CANDICE. We've all read your books before joining the class. You know freaking Cornel West and Michael Eric Dyson. You've been a pundit on CNN and MSNBC. You're not afraid to call out white supremacy in the simplest of ways and you don't even make white people feel bad when you do it. It's brilliant. You're like, a badass.

SANDRA. Candice, I'm just a professor. As much yours as Malik's as anyone else.

CANDICE. Got it.

SANDRA. Good.

CANDICE. But can I ask you a question Professor?

SANDRA. Please.

CANDICE. Isn't it hard though? Being a woman in academia. You seem so strong and resilient. It's almost like you're inhuman. How do you do it?

> (**SANDRA** *is grounded by this question. It sort of takes the wind out of her unexpectedly. She sits on her desk and stares into the abyss for answers.*)

Professor?

SANDRA. Inhuman.

CANDICE. Or maybe superhuman? Superwoman?

SANDRA. God. Is that what you see?

CANDICE. I mean, like I meant that as a compliment. I don't know how to be that tough. I cry in my really abbreviated ten-minute showers. I'm ashamed to say that out loud to my girls. Like women can't be progressive and also be sensitive or whatever. Especially over a dude. Like I'm basically setting us back a lot of feminism years with every tear I shed, and totally should keep it repressed at all times. But like – how do you do that?

SANDRA. You're asking me?

CANDICE. You know a lot of things.

SANDRA. I don't know that. Why would you think I know that? Why would you think I don't have pain or shed tears?

CANDICE. Because like...you don't *seem* to.

(**SANDRA** *releases an audible sigh. Clearly disturbed.*)

Did I say something to...offend –

SANDRA. I'm fine.

(*A beat.*)

Actually, Candice, it is hard. It is very very hard to be a woman in academia. A Black woman, even harder. I have to temper myself with my colleagues. With my students. I feel that I owe something to myself, to women, to...the future, even, to make sure that I am not disposable here. And that means carrying myself with a demeanor that doesn't allow for much crack in the foundation.

CANDICE. What a serious drag. When do you get to be real?

SANDRA. It's only a drag when you're in the middle of a divorce. That, Candice, is a bonafide drag. Because a ten-minute shower or a twenty-minute shower or even thirty minutes in a jacuzzi cannot wash off the funk of a failed marriage. Especially when it's possibly your fault. And your husband can't understand what it means for you to be a working woman even when he says he does, you know?

CANDICE. Totally know it.

SANDRA. I shattered the glass ceiling and didn't keep a man in the process. What a cliché. And yet, I pick myself up and come to work because I am doing something greater than myself. To see a young woman like you begin to own her white privilege is a sign for me to carry on. My work matters.

CANDICE. It definitely does.

SANDRA. Now I have a question for you.

CANDICE. For me?

SANDRA. Were you organizing my office yesterday after hours?

CANDICE. Not too late. Why do you ask?

SANDRA. Curious if any of the students who wanted office hours came by.

CANDICE. Is this about the picture on your door?

SANDRA. Did you see anyone stop by?

CANDICE. I think that's disgusting that someone would do that.

SANDRA. Perhaps a disgruntled student of some sort?

CANDICE. I didn't see.

SANDRA. And what time did you finish in my office yesterday?

CANDICE. I was clearing desktop files until about 5:30 p.m. Then I had to get to study group at six so I split.

SANDRA. Got it.

CANDICE. But I locked up like always. Put the keys in the mailbox like you trained me to do.

SANDRA. Okay, thank you.

> (*An awkward moment.* **SANDRA** *begins to sort through papers on her desk. She can feel* **CANDICE**'s *eyes boring through her. Looks up at her.*)

SANDRA. Yeessss?

CANDICE. That wasn't like...an accusation question, right?

SANDRA. Accusation?

CANDICE. About me?

SANDRA. It was just for clarity.

CANDICE. Because like...I really respect you. A lot. And have been working really hard to prove to you that I belong here. I know a lot of the other students wanted this position. And I have no idea why you chose me, actually, but I appreciate it.

SANDRA. And you do good work. I made a great decision.

CANDICE. And I'd never do anything to like... I mean that was disgusting.

SANDRA. Okay, Candice. You've made your point. I was just wondering if you had seen anything out of the ordinary. You said you didn't and I believe you.

CANDICE. What do you think that was about?

SANDRA. I have no idea. Someone might've been upset about a grade. Or...didn't like the essay topic I handed out about the effects of the slave trade on modern civilization.

CANDICE. Like someone thought you shouldn't be talking about slavery?

SANDRA. Perhaps they found it offensive. Or it triggered some sense of guilt.

CANDICE. Or was it your Black Lives Matter shirt?

(SANDRA *looks at* CANDICE.)

SANDRA. What's that?

CANDICE. I know some students had a problem with you wearing it. Totally not addressing their unconscious racism.

SANDRA. What would my BLM shirt have to do with a picture of a slave woman and a white baby suckling her breast?

CANDICE. I just know some people are stupid. Maybe your shirt made them feel uncomfortable and they felt like making you feel uncomfortable? Maybe they felt like you were reminding them of their privilege in a way that didn't feel respectful or considerate. Maybe they just wanted you to see an image of how things used to be to like remind you of...

(SANDRA *eyes* CANDICE *cautiously.*)

SANDRA. My place?

(CANDICE *is still. Uncomfortable.*)

CANDICE. I don't really know. I found the whole thing, woman to woman, completely offensive.

(SANDRA *studies* CANDICE *a beat longer.* CANDICE *can barely breathe. Have they crossed a dangerous point here?*)

(*Finally:*)

SANDRA. It's almost time for my last class. I'm going to need to head out.

CANDICE. Do you want me to finish decorating your board? I have a whole section of red Post-its that need your attention.

SANDRA. I've reached my Post-it limit for the day. Let's save that for tomorrow.

CANDICE. Cool. No prob.

(CANDICE *grabs a backpack as* SANDRA *watches her like a hawk. She heads to the door.*)

SANDRA. Keep in mind, Candice, I can always put in a word for you to get an additional stipend to offset your financial aid deficit. Always willing to support my students-in-need. Should you find yourself in a tight jam.

> (**CANDICE** *looks at* **SANDRA**. *Is that a power play? A threat? She decides not to push it.*)

CANDICE. Thank you, Professor. You're the absolute best.

> (*And she leaves. Lights shift.*)

6.

(Lights up on **SARA** *in Master's office in the big house. She dusts around the corners of a grand desk. Sees a parchment folded on the desk. She pulls another blank parchment from the desk and begins to copy what she sees on the parchment. Hears a noise and sets down the pen nervously. Folds the parchment into her breast quickly.)*

*(***LUANNE**, *another Black woman servant, enters the office. Stops, a bit startled at the sight of* **SARA**.*)*

LUANNE. Sara, sweet Jesus. I wunn't expecting no company. What you doin' in here?

SARA. Cleanin'. What it look like?

LUANNE. But you ain't no house nigger.

SARA. Neither is you but here you is.

LUANNE. I'm s'pose to be the one who do Master's office. He put me here hisself.

SARA. Well then, LuAnne, you musta been reassigned. I do it now. On assignment from Missy Sue.

LUANNE. Missy Sue, that right?

SARA. That's right.

LUANNE. She back for good? Thought maybe this was only a visit.

SARA. Who knows? But this where she want me so this where I am. And I don't wants to do a bad job and ruin the good legacy of a clean office that you done built with your hand. So if you'll excuse me, I'm gon' get back to it.

(LUANNE *watches* SARA *clean around the desk.* SARA *moves to the curtains to make herself less obvious. Picks up specks of dust.*)

LUANNE. He likes when you iron the curtains. Gon' have to take 'em down and steam 'em out back.

SARA. I'll get to that later.

LUANNE. And the desk drawers creak if you don't put some oil to 'em. He get real perturbed by the creakin'.

SARA. Thanks for the tips.

LUANNE. Just want you to do a good job. Lots of rewards for good jobs. Might get you a extra biscuit for supper.

SARA. *(Sarcasm.)* Well that'll make the whole thing worth it.

(*A pause.* LUANNE *studies* SARA.)

LUANNE. Where she got you sleeping?

SARA. Pardon me?

LUANNE. You sleeping here in the big house? Or she put you back in the field after supper?

SARA. I sleep in the straw bed I done always slept in. Back in my cabin.

LUANNE. Well I guess they can't have two of us darkies in the big house overnight. Probably makes 'em too anxious.

SARA. You sleep here in the big house?

LUANNE. Since few days ago. Master improved my conditions.

SARA. I'll bet he did.

LUANNE. It's good to see a friend in here, Sara. Ain't none of these other kitchen-hands nice to me at all. You'd think they done plumb forgot we all slave kin. But tha's how it go, I guess. Envy ain't never been good for the soul.

SARA. LuAnne, who in they rightful mind got envy for you?

LUANNE. What you meanin' by that?

SARA. You a slave from the field who keep Master's bed warm and done worked yo' way into a full-time position at it. Who you figure wanna trade places? I think you gon' be a undisputed champ on that one.

LUANNE. Don't be ugly to me Sara. You ugly enough as it is without doin' nothin' extra.

SARA. Seem to me ugly is preferable. Pretty is the last thing I want Master to think of me. But that's just my guess from the outside lookin' in.

LUANNE. Why you gotta be mean and hateful? I was trying to be pleasant witcha. Even though you taken my tasks and get me reassigned behind my back.

SARA. I ain't get you reassigned. I done already told you that's Missy Sue.

LUANNE. Oh everybody know Missy Sue do whatever you say. We seein' the way she look at you.

SARA. *(Intrigued.)* Lookin' at me? What you talkin' about?

LUANNE. Like the way a woman look at her husband who done come back for her with his freedom papers in his hand. I seen that only one time in my life and the feeling it gave me was like happiness and passion and excitement all in one. Like if that woman ain't run into that man's arms and jump his bones right there, I'da did it for her. And that look...that's what Missy Sue give you.

SARA. You talk crazier than a slave with the fever.

LUANNE. She got fever for you. I seen it.

(**SARA** *is intrigued again. Is this possible?*)

SARA. That ain't even part of our nature. It like...we ain't s'posed to even think like that.

(LUANNE sniffs SARA's curiosity.)

LUANNE. Nature ain't no slave. It move to its own rhythm. Ain't you never been tempted by that rhythm, Sara?

SARA. The good book tell you what rhythm to move by.

LUANNE. Nature don't care 'bout yo' good book. Nature its own god. I done felt a nature that no words can describe. I bet not even yo' good book could translate it.

SARA. I'm pretty sho it translate to the devil.

LUANNE. And who do it say is the devil again? I forget. The master or the slave?

(SARA rolls her eyes at LUANNE.)

Yo' good book tell you to be a good slave and you obey it. It tell you to feel thangs and never move on them feelin's. It say only masters get to act on they passions. But what about the slaves? I say you can keep yo' book and I'll stick with nature.

SARA. Why don't you go to nature right now and leave me to my task?

LUANNE. Why you so quick to get rid of me Sara?

SARA. I don't likes to work with distractions.

LUANNE. Then tell me why you here and I'll leave you be.

SARA. I told you, I been reassigned.

LUANNE. Why you been reassigned? What you after?

SARA. Who say I got to be after something? I ain't you. Everything ain't about getting outta the field for me.

LUANNE. You thank all I'm 'bout is trying to get outta the field?

SARA. If the shuck 'n' cluckin' you do ain't about gettin' outta the field, then whassit for?

LUANNE. I ain't no shuck 'n' cluck.

SARA. Whatever you say.

LUANNE. You ain't got to act too proud and mighty, Sara. You knew what was good for you, you'd take that passion Missy Sue got and turn it to your advantage. What I got wit' Master, you got with Missy. We ain't nothin' but two sides of the same looking glass.

SARA. Only I ain't here for no improved conditions.

LUANNE. Then what you here for?

> (SARA *catches herself.* LUANNE *is about to make her get sloppy. She pulls back. Goes to scrutinize the curtains again.*)

SARA. Say he like to have these ironed?

LUANNE. Once a week, at least.

SARA. Then I better start takin' 'em down.

LUANNE. You wants some help?

SARA. What you want for the help you gon' give?

LUANNE. Damn Sara! Can't even take a helping hand without no insults to my fine character. You think I ain't the same as you? You think I done forgot?

SARA. I wouldn't know, LuAnne.

LUANNE. Admit it, Sara. You ain't never liked nor trusted me.

SARA. Seem like you just admitted it for me.

LUANNE. Why you that way to me?

SARA. I don't know.

> (LUANNE *walks over to* SARA *at the desk. She sits at its edge.* SARA *moves the parchment slowly away from* LUANNE, *so as not to crumple it.*)

LUANNE. I know y'all say thangs 'bout me in the field. Think I'm weak cuz I take to Master's bed. Think I've sold my soul to the devil in yo' good book. But my mama used to be a steel rod woman, you remember that?

SARA. 'Course. I ain't never forgot Mama Mabel. She taught me to tend to the sicknesses and birth babies after my own mama got hung. Your maw carried a lil' piece of all of us. Fed me and Abner like we was her own. Your mama was steel rod fa sho.

LUANNE. I seen her with a bunch of babies suckling her breast all my life. Seen her feed Missy Sue. Seen her feed all them bastard chir'ren Master brought back for her to tend to. We be in the cabin hungry, scrappin' over grains of rice cuz she sharin' her satchel with you and Abner and every other slave child.

SARA. Your mama was as pure as they come.

LUANNE. She died right here on this plantation, and so long as she was alive, ain't none of us never got whipped nor branded. She kept us safe. Made us kin. But what we do when she leave? We put her in the ground and we keep on bein' slaves. No kinda kin. Ain't nothin' change. Life she give us better than most on other plantations. And still, when we die, we just slaves in the ground.

SARA. We ain't got to die slaves.

LUANNE. I know you see me as disgracing my mama for all she done to keep us free of harm. But what I see is looking for another way to have something. And what I give up to Master is easier than lettin' him sneak down here and take it from me anyway.

'Least I feel like I'm giving somethin' over that I own myself. And if it's leaving me, it's leaving borrowed, not stolen.

SARA. I guess you do what you do LuAnne. If it workin', who am I to say it ain't right?

LUANNE. But you still don't trust me, right? Still don't see me as your kin?

> (**SARA** *looks at* **LUANNE.** *Uncertain of what to say.*)

Tell me what you plannin', Sara. Is you runnin' away?

SARA. I ain't got no plans.

LUANNE. I wants to come with you.

SARA. I told you I ain't got no plans.

LUANNE. What you doin' in here cleanin'? You gon' steal from Master?

SARA. I ain't no thief. It's against the good book.

LUANNE. I think you only use that good book when it's favorable and ignore it when it ain't.

SARA. Maybe but it's my business to do so and not yours.

LUANNE. Tell me Sara. Tell me what you doin' cuz I know it ain't just cleanin'. I hear talk of insurrection. I hear talk of runnin' away. Everybody getting extra courage in them cuz of this fight goin' on. Talking of gettin' free in a hundred different ways. I believe you one of them folk with ideas. 'Fore yo' brother run away, he musta done put some freedom talk into you too. You ain't gone go and leave the rest of us behind, is ya?

SARA. Naw LuAnne, I ain't.

LUANNE. Then tell me. Kin to kin. I can help ya.

> (**SARA** *eyes* **LUANNE** *carefully for signs of trust. Then suddenly, she has a second thought.*)

SARA. LuAnne, can you read?

LUANNE. It's illegal to read.

SARA. That ain't what I asked ya.

LUANNE. Ain't nobody never learned me how to read.

SARA. What if I taught ya? Would you wanna learn?

LUANNE. Is you sayin' *you* can read???

SARA. I ain't sayin' that. I'm asking would you wanna learn?

LUANNE. 'Course.

SARA. Even if it ain't easy.

LUANNE. Still.

SARA. Even if it's illegal and can get you caught?

LUANNE. Even if.

SARA. I can't tell you I'm doin' nothin' here besides cleanin'. That's what Missy Sue asked me to do. But ifn you learn to read, you be real useful to freedom, if that's what you want.

LUANNE. You sayin' reading gonna make me free?

(**LUANNE** *looks at* **SARA**. *They are both still uncertain of the other's intentions.*)

SARA. LuAnne, yo mama taught us one way to survive. My mama taught us another. But we also learn on our own, ain't we? I'm bettin' we put all our ways together, we can figure out how to get to freedom. If you wants to read, I can get Missy Sue to learn you is all I'm sayin'.

LUANNE. Alright. I wants to learn.

SARA. Good then. You will.

(*A smile between them. Almost friendly.*)

Now let me get to cleanin' on my own. I got to prove myself worthy of my new assignment.

LUANNE. Alright Sara. Don't forget about the curtains. And the desk drawers. And he likes a bit of tea waiting for him in the evening.

SARA. Gotcha.

(**LUANNE** *heads out of the office.*)

And LuAnne, if you tell anybody what I just promised you, I'll kill you in your sleep.

(**LUANNE** *looks at* **SARA** *in terror. Nods. And leaves.*)

7.

(Lights up on **SANDRA** *in her office, listening to smooth jazz through her desk speakers.* She pulls the shade to the door of her office before pouring herself a glass of wine and taking off her shoes. The day has been long.)*

(A tap at the door. **JADE** *[same actress who plays* **LUANNE***] peeks in at* **SANDRA***.)*

JADE. Sandra, got a minute?

SANDRA. Sure.

> *(***SANDRA*** sits up and turns down her music, trying to mask her disappointment and annoyance.)*

JADE. Hope I'm not intruding.

SANDRA. Just winding down for the day.

JADE. Been a mutha, hunh?

SANDRA. Putting it mildly.

JADE. Has the university given you any more information about the incident?

SANDRA. Not much.

JADE. These students ought to seriously know better. This isn't high school.

SANDRA. Apparently it is.

JADE. It continues to go unchecked because Dean Whitfield allows it to. The professors of color barely get the respect

---

*A license to produce *Confederates* does not include a performance license for any third-party or copyrighted music. Licensees should create an original composition or use music in the public domain. For further information, please see the Music and Third-Party Materials Use Note on page iii.

we deserve but we're expected to be these "tolerant negroes." Meanwhile these kids get a simple slap on the wrist. They'll call it "mischief," knowing good and damn well that those same rules would not apply if the students weren't white.

SANDRA. I'm not sure it was a white student that did it.

(JADE *laughs with a smirk.*)

JADE. Right.

SANDRA. No, I'm serious.

JADE. Un-huh.

(JADE *looks at* SANDRA. *She's serious. Not worth going there with her in this moment.*)

SANDRA. So you wanted something...

JADE. I wanted to talk to you about tenure.

SANDRA. You know we're not allowed to fully discuss –

JADE. I know the rules. I don't want to "fully discuss." I just want to let you know, as a tenured faculty member yourself, how much I value your presence here at this university. I've taken after your footsteps in a way. You've always been an inspiration to me.

SANDRA. Wow, Jade. I didn't know you felt that way. I'm flattered.

JADE. I know we don't chat much, which is actually a shame considering there's only a handful of us here. It's clear that we come from different world views, obviously.

SANDRA. Okay. Obviously.

JADE. I just mean that you've been a part of a pedigreed educational track from the beginning. I switched here after seven years of teaching community college. It's a different journey.

SANDRA. Well, sure.

JADE. But still, your accomplishments are nothing to dismiss. Your publications in *Princeton Review* and *Arts and Letters.* You've blazed an admirable path and I commend you sister.

SANDRA. Thank you Jade. I appreciate the pick-me-up after the day I've had.

JADE. You're welcome.

(She takes a minute. Hesitates.)

I wasn't sure if I should do this.

SANDRA. Do what exactly?

JADE. I want to remain professional, obviously.

SANDRA. You concerned about tenure?

JADE. I know all of the tenured professors have to vote on whether or not I advance.

SANDRA. It's just a standard formality. You should be fine.

JADE. Except...and forgive me for being obtuse, but I've heard some things and I want to make sure that we don't have any strangeness between us.

SANDRA. Things like what?

JADE. I've heard from other faculty that I shouldn't count on a vote from you.

SANDRA. Uh-huh.

JADE. And I don't mean to cross a line, because obviously you've a right to your own assessment, but I have to say that if that's true, I think it's pretty fucked up.

SANDRA. Oh. Okay. Alright. Okay.

JADE. I'm not trying to be confrontational.

SANDRA. Just cursed at me.

JADE. That's just me being relaxed. There's room for casualness right? After hours?

SANDRA. I guess.

JADE. I would be negligent if I didn't express myself to you.

SANDRA. And where did you get the idea that I wouldn't vote for you?

JADE. I don't think that's important. I don't want to cause friction between you and other colleagues.

SANDRA. Clearly there's already friction.

JADE. It's not throwing shade. It's just real talk.

SANDRA. And what is this real talk?

JADE. That you seemed hesitant about co-signing me and my work.

SANDRA. As an educator?

JADE. I'm not sure. My sources weren't completely transparent. Which is why I figured I'd come straight to you. Out of respect.

SANDRA. Respect.

JADE. If you have doubts about my credentials, I wish you would just say so now.

SANDRA. I don't have those doubts. Why would I have those doubts?

JADE. I don't know. I just know it happens sometimes.

SANDRA. What happens sometimes?

JADE. When there are more than one...you know what I'm saying...there can be some sense of rivalry. You know how it goes.

SANDRA. You think I'm being a crab in a barrel? I'm afraid of you getting ahead so I'm trying to pull you back under? Is that it?

JADE. Not quite a crab in a barrel.

SANDRA. Not quite???

JADE. I don't like what I heard. Like I said, I think it's fucked up. If it's true. I don't want this divide and conquer thing going on between the only two of us in this department. But if you felt that way, I want to know why.

SANDRA. I don't know what to say to you Jade. I'm sort of speechless.

JADE. Do you deny it?

SANDRA. I can't even... I don't know where to begin.

JADE. You can begin with a yes or no.

SANDRA. I don't like this interrogation.

JADE. It's not an interrogation. It's just a question. Colleague to colleague. Sister to sister.

(SANDRA *snorts in spite of herself.*)

SANDRA. Sister to sister?

JADE. Oh I'm sorry. Should I not call you that?

SANDRA. You said yourself we barely spend time with one another. It's just, loosely used, perhaps.

JADE. I'm speaking beyond the interpersonal.

SANDRA. Yeah, I get that.

JADE. That's not your deal though, hunh?

SANDRA. Now you're questioning something else.

JADE. It's my job to question everything and encourage the same in my students. Just like you.

SANDRA. We have very different ways of engaging the students, actually.

JADE. See, now what does that mean?

SANDRA. It means your methods are different than mine. We're different educators.

JADE. Meaning you're superior and I'm inferior?

SANDRA. I would never say that.

JADE. But you're using the word different like a divider. I can hear it in your context. You have a judgment about the way that I teach.

SANDRA. It's not my style. That's not a judgment. It's just a difference.

JADE. What is *my* style, exactly?

SANDRA. You're a lot more coddling than I am.

JADE. Coddling?

SANDRA. It's a stylistic choice.

JADE. Who do I coddle?

SANDRA. Malik Powers, for one.

JADE. Malik Powers? The one Black male student in our department? You've got to be kidding me.

SANDRA. He always seems to be in your office. It seems he gets a lot of extra time from you.

JADE. I could say the same about you.

SANDRA. I engage his critical thinking. But no more than the other students.

JADE. Are you sure this isn't because Malik actually likes my class? That he and I have a close relationship? That perhaps your distance from him is a case of... *(Pause.)*

SANDRA. Well don't stop there. Please finish the / statement –

JADE. Jealousy.

SANDRA. And what would I be jealous of exactly?

JADE. That the Black students here seem to feel more nurtured by me than by you.

SANDRA. You're speaking for all of the Black students? Because there are six here. Malik isn't the only one.

JADE. All of the others have expressed a sense of being polarized here. And that I'm the only one who gets them.

SANDRA. I get them.

JADE. It's not a competition, Sandra.

SANDRA. No it isn't, Jade.

(A beat. The women politely fume at each other.)

JADE. Sandra, I'm disappointed in the direction of our conversation. I was hoping for a window into understanding you more interpersonally.

SANDRA. That why you started with accusations?

JADE. Again, not accusing. Just questioning.

SANDRA. Okay. Questioning.

JADE. I know we come from different backgrounds.

SANDRA. You make sure to keep bringing that up.

JADE. It has some meaning.

SANDRA. It also has judgment.

JADE. That's just how you're hearing it.

SANDRA. No, it's also how you're saying it. You keep making the distinction between your side of the tracks and mine. That I'm from this elitism and you're from the people. That somehow the Black students connect more with you because you spent seven years in community college and you come from their world and therefore you're more down and I'm just another "tolerant negro" professor that's absorbed in the system of institutional racism. That's what you're saying in those distinctions. If we really want to get real, let's get all the way real.

(*Pause.*)

JADE. There are a lot of things that I want to say to that but I'm trying to remain professional.

SANDRA. We're past professional.

JADE. Well then, you know what sister? Let's be all the way real. When I first came to this university, many teachers opened up their homes to me, took me to lunch, invited me to dinners with their families. You? Nothing. Ever. You don't think that *you're* the one drawing lines? What kind of sister doesn't look out for her own?

SANDRA. Look out for you how?! Invite you to my home? My home that was falling apart for years before my divorce settled in? You want to have dinner with me and my husband? Talk about our problems with intimacy and our different career tracks and the fact that we couldn't conceive? That the dinner you were missing out on? If I unraveled to you and ripped out what was barely left of my dignity would that have made you feel more connected to me? God forbid we both be Black and I don't unravel in front of you. Because maybe, just maybe, I wouldn't be able to thread myself back together again. And while you're feeling good about us both having some sense of kinship, what the hell am I supposed to do with scattered fucking threads of myself???

(*Silence.* **JADE** *is speechless. Unable to figure out the next appropriate move.* **SANDRA** *tries to breathe.*)

(*Then, finally:*)

JADE. I overstepped. I see that.

(**SANDRA** *lets out an audible sigh in response. Almost a bitter laugh.*)

JADE. I came here to this university because I wanted to earn prestige as an educator. But I also came here because I knew we were underrepresented here. I remember when I was in Ivy League education and the only person of color in my class. Always feeling like my professors had a bias against me. They belonged to the other students who they shared a cultural background with. I never had that. And the one time a Black woman came to my department from Spelman College, I thought – yes, finally. Someone here to see me and take me under her wing. But she was so tough on the few students of color that we ended up hating her more than anybody.

We hated this Black woman professor because she didn't just disappoint us. She rejected us as her kin. I never want to do that to my students. I want to be available to the Black students at a White university and let them know that I am here for you. Because being isolated almost destroyed me.

    (Beat.)

SANDRA. So...

JADE. Is this why you don't think I'm suitable for tenure? Because I center my Black students?

SANDRA. I never said you weren't suitable for tenure. I may have mentioned in casual conversation that it'd be nice to see you evolve in your relationships with your students –

JADE. That's not something you could tell me directly?

SANDRA. I don't think this is a good idea. We're allowing things said by others to color our perspective of each other. It's dangerous territory and will get irreversible.

JADE. Fair enough.

SANDRA. I never said I wouldn't co-sign you. I can only make a recommendation anyway. It's not my decision. There's an entire hierarchy –

JADE. Understood.

(She heads to the door.)

I respect your position. Thank you for allowing me a moment of indulgence. I hope you have a good evening.

SANDRA. Jade.

JADE. Yes?

SANDRA. Students speak to you...about me?

JADE. That's not something I –

SANDRA. I mentioned a white student might not've put this on my door and you laughed.

JADE. I've seen a lot of crimes go unpunished on this campus. Still not fair of me to assume.

SANDRA. Right. But none of them alluded to this? Confided in you, by any chance?

JADE. If they did, what are you...you'd ask me to betray something they shared with me in confidence?

SANDRA. I would think...if it were something like this...

JADE. Of course.

(A pause. The women look at each other carefully.)

I didn't put a sign on your door, Sandra. It's not my style.

SANDRA. No, I wouldn't suggest that.

JADE. Good.

SANDRA. But I think you might really know who did.

(JADE looks at SANDRA incredulously.)

JADE. When you wore your Black Lives Matter shirt to work the other day, I was proud. For once, just in that nine-hour workday, it felt like we were actually sisters. And not everybody felt that way.

(*She opens the door to the office.*)

Have a good evening.

(**SANDRA** *looks at the door as* **JADE** *walks through it. The door shuts firmly.*)

8.

(Lights up on **SARA** *and* **ABNER** *in Sara's cabin.* **SARA** *fingers a musket while* **ABNER** *eats a bowl of grits, masticating the food aggressively. Been missing a good meal.)*

SARA. They must ain't feedin' you good in them swamps.

ABNER. Can't compare to yo' grits. I told you got to support the bottom wit' yo' other hand.

SARA. Like this?

*(***SARA** *makes an attempt.)*

ABNER. You hold that like you almost know what you doin'.

SARA. You get to kill anybody yet?

ABNER. What kinda question is that Sara?

SARA. A real one.

ABNER. You say it like the thought of it give you thrills. Ain't no thrill in seeing a man with his guts bleeding out into the soil.

SARA. Seen it 'least ten times with slaves what been whipped so bad looked like their skin came alive and was crawling on they own flesh.

ABNER. I'm eatin' / Sara.

SARA. Coupla of 'em died right befo' me. Seen it when they lynched George's boy few seasons past. Why death all a sudden make you squirm when it's the slave master?

ABNER. Ain't said I was squirming. Just say ain't no thrill about it. Ain't no thrill in none of it.

SARA. But has you killed yet?

ABNER. No.

SARA. Come too close to it? Got any battle scars?

ABNER. Naw, I ain't got no scars.

SARA. Why come you ain't? What they got you doin' out there in battle if you ain't killin'?

ABNER. Told you killin' ain't all to war. Gots lot of duties. Who you thank loading them artillery carriages? Shuttlin' them muskets in them wagons from point to point? Helping to build them log roads over them swamps?

SARA. That's what you out there doin'?

ABNER. That and then some.

SARA. What's the glory in that? Sound like mo' slave work.

ABNER. Ain't no slave work. You takes that back.

SARA. Sound like slave work to me. Is you getting paid?

ABNER. Getting paid in freedom papers.

SARA. Ha! That's some trickery. You just contraband. I hear them callin' you that in Master Dan's office when he be talkin' to his confederates.

ABNER. His who?

SARA. His white kin what be on his same side. Like they all wants the same things...fo' yo' Black ass to keep shufflin' and haulin' without never reapin' nothin' for yo'self.

ABNER. Hope you ain't bein' too nosy in there with Master Dan. S'pose to gather the map points he done plotted out for his troops and pass 'em over.

SARA. I'm a good dispatch. Master Dan don't hardly notice me in there cleanin' and tidyin' like I do. I may as well be the wall paint. He say everything they plannin' like it ain't nothin'. What swamps they movin' into. Which troops got which artillery and where. Even speak so free as to discuss the Proclamation.

ABNER. What he sayin'?

SARA. Say that Ol' White Man with the tall hat done signed somethin' called pre-lim-in-ary.

ABNER. What's that meanin'?

SARA. Meanin' us folks gonna be able to sign up for the war without hiding. The law gonna make it so. And we be all gettin' free.

ABNER. You wrote that down so's I can take it to my general?

SARA. 'Course I wrote it down. Master Dan don't think nothin' of a darkee woman. Figure we only got enough sense to feed they babies and shine they floors. Never figurin' I'm writing down everything I remember, and I remember everything.

ABNER. And you sho' ain't nobody onto ya?

SARA. LuAnne is a bit snoopy, but I got her under control.

ABNER. LuAnne? She couldn't hold hot pee on a cold day if her freedom depended on it. What you trusting her fo'?

SARA. I told you I got her under control. She my kin now.

ABNER. Yo' kin? What that got to do with trust?

SARA. I done got Missy Sue to learn her to read. Now she in as much trouble with the law as you an' me. Tha's how we stay even.

ABNER. Readin' a get her whipped. What you and me doin' get us swingin' from that great oak.

(*A noise outside the cabin.* **ABNER** *jumps.*)

Quick, hide that thang!

(**SARA** *hides the musket. Goes over to the door and peers outside.*)

SARA. Just Missy Sue.

ABNER. Then I ain't got to hide.

SARA. Can't be too certain. Just stay in that hatch.

(**MISSY SUE** *enters, and* **SARA** *shuts the door tightly behind her.*)

MISSY SUE. Father's been asking questions.

SARA. 'Bout who? You or me?

MISSY SUE. Wanted to know if you might've told me anything, Sara. About Abner's whereabouts.

SARA. Tell him no, ain't you?

MISSY SUE. I have. We'll have to move quickly now. Father's getting suspicious of our closeness. He hasn't a clue about our dispatching to the Union, but he is concerned about Abner. I know he's due back here tonight. Has he arrived?

SARA. Not yet Missy.

MISSY SUE. Well then we still have time.

(**MISSY SUE** *starts unbuttoning her blouse.*)

SARA. What you doin' there Missy? I can pardon you if you needs to undress –

MISSY SUE. Relax yourself, Sara.

(**MISSY SUE** *is now removing her corset.* **SARA** *doesn't know whether to watch or run. She turns her face but peeks back here and there.*)

(*Beneath* **MISSY SUE***'s corset is a map taped across her ribs. She removes the map and hands it to* **SARA.***)*

For you to pass to Abner. When he arrives.

(**SARA** *turns back away and* **MISSY SUE**, *nearly naked from the waist up, touches* **SARA***'s face and turns it back to hers.*)

You don't have to look away.

SARA. It's indecent, Missy.

MISSY SUE. We're living in indecent times, Sara.

SARA. Shouldn't be here when Abner arrives Missy. Best if you keep your father distracted.

MISSY SUE. Have you thought of what you'll do?

SARA. What's that?

MISSY SUE. When it's time to leave this plantation.

SARA. Just figure I get free first and figure the rest out after then.

MISSY SUE. You don't have to worry about that if you come with me. I'll take care of you.

SARA. You mean like a husband take care of his wife?

> (**MISSY SUE** *smiles. She caresses* **SARA***'s face.* **SARA** *tries not to enjoy it, though she does a bit.*)

MISSY SUE. I want you to come with me. Speak before a council of abolitionists. Your story will spread empathy for our cause. I feel passionately connected to you, Sara. Do you feel it?

> (**SARA** *breathes rapidly, her body defying all rules.*)

SARA. Good book say only a master get to act on they passion. But what about the slave? What must it be to do the taking steada bein' took, huh Missy?

> (**SARA** *looks at* **MISSY SUE** *in her near-nakedness. She can't help herself. She's aroused.*)
>
> (*She grabs* **MISSY SUE** *and kisses her feverishly. She pushes her toward the bed.* **SARA** *is in control here.*)

(Suddenly, a noise from outside. They both jump.)

*(**SARA** quickly remembers herself. Rushes over to the door.)*

SARA. Someone's out there, Missy. You best get gone now!

*(**MISSY SUE** grabs her clothing and tries to quickly redress.)*

MISSY SUE. Oh, Sara, that was...really aggressive of you, wasn't it?

SARA. Musta been all that freedom talk, Missy. I forgot myself. Come on nah, go'on.

*(**MISSY SUE** is a bit bewildered by their encounter. She is suddenly not the one in control. She attempts to regain composure, and status.)*

MISSY SUE. Well I um...yes. Remember what I say about the council, Sara. I can help you get free.

SARA. My freedom's coming whether they like it or not, ain't it Missy?

*(**MISSY SUE** leaves, unsettled. **ABNER** pokes his head out of the closet as **SARA** continues to watch carefully outside.)*

ABNER. The hell was you doin' on her –

SARA. Shhhh!!! Stay in that hatch! Somebody out there!

*(**ABNER** ducks his head back into the closet. **SARA** finally grabs a candle. Looks out into the night. Sees **LUANNE**.)*

LuAnne, what you doin' out here?

LUANNE. Need to talk to you Sara.

SARA. Well talk.

> (**LUANNE** *tries to peer inside the cabin.*)

LUANNE. You ain't gon' let me inside?

SARA. I'm cookin' pigs' feet 'n' grits. Stank somethin' awful.

LUANNE. Please Sara! I could get lynched for what I got to say.

> (**SARA** *hesitates. Then finally she opens wider for* **LUANNE** *to enter.*)

SARA. Make it quick.

> (**LUANNE** *looks around the cabin. Very cautiously. Then turns to* **SARA** *pointedly.*)

LUANNE. Missy Sue gone?

SARA. You just seen her, ain't you. Why?

LUANNE. I'm gon' kill Master Dan.

SARA. You gon' what?

LUANNE. Grind some glass in his grits.

SARA. What you talkin' 'bout LuAnne?

LUANNE. I can do it real easy. All that fine china they got in the dining room. Or I can do it in his wine cup when he settle down for a nightcap.

SARA. What got you talkin' crazy like this?

LUANNE. He done sold me.

SARA. To who?

LUANNE. Whitfield Acres. Way downward from here some hundred miles, they say.

SARA. You can't kill Master Dan.

LUANNE. I can and I will. He done took me and took me 'til I has nothin' left, and then throw me out like scraps cuz he done found another one younger 'n' me.

SARA. Who he done found?

LUANNE. Cora Mae. Young gal from the Beeker farm.

SARA. She ain't but twelve years.

LUANNE. Done put her in the house. Ain't room for alla us in one house, he say. Try to get me to wrastle her for it. I tolds him no. He say then I'm gettin' sold to Whitfield Acres.

SARA. He just scarin' you.

LUANNE. I can't be gettin' on no other plantation. I done did everything here. I'm s'pose to reap my harvest. I ain't s'pose to be gettin' robbed.

SARA. You can't kill.

LUANNE. I'm is. And then I'm fleein' for the Union. Gon' make myself contraband.

SARA. What you know 'bout contraband?

LUANNE. I know that's what yo' brother is. And I know he in here somewheres. Been standing out there all night and watch him run up in here. Right before Missy Sue come to tempt devil feelings in you.

SARA. I don't know what you talkin' LuAnne.

LUANNE. No point wasting no time Sara. I knowin' he here and I'm gon' tell you what. I wants him to take me wit' him when he leave tonight.

SARA. I don't know what you –

LUANNE. Else I'm tellin' Master Dan you been stealing his plans and passing 'em to the Union.

(SARA *looks at* LUANNE *sternly. This chick is smarter than she thought.*)

SARA. You sneaky lil' cotton picker. You been plannin' this all along, ain't you?

(**LUANNE** *shrugs.* **ABNER** *opens up the closet and walks out.*)

Abner! Don't!

ABNER. I'll take you.

SARA. You can't take her! She ain't to be trusted.

LUANNE. I'm is Sara. I just needs me collateral. Just like you.

SARA. You a sneak!

LUANNE. I'm only doin' what's necessary. We all gots to do what's necessary.

ABNER. But Sara got to come now too. Ain't none of us can be here wıt Master's blood on the soil. We all be hung.

SARA. This ain't what I want! Tired of bein' tugged this way and that when ain't none of y'all got direction. I wants freedom by my own deliverance. I 'on't want no blood on my hands 'less it's for the war.

LUANNE. This too be a war. This for my own blood bein' spilt. This for me not bein' no scrap nigger to be bought and sold no more. This too be a war.

ABNER. Seem like y'all both been tookin' – one by Master, the other by his offspring. Our mark is when the last cabin light go out. Ain't none of us gon' be no scrap niggers no mo'.

LUANNE. What we gon' do about Missy Sue?

(**ABNER** *looks at* **SARA**. **SARA** *pulls out the musket from hiding. An unapologetic leader now.*)

SARA. Whatever's necessary. I'm gon' carry this. Cuz I knows they ain't give this to you, Abner. You done stole it, sho nuff. Ain't no niggers gettin' armed by the white man. Even ones on the side of the Union. We on our own side now.

ABNER. You hold it then. We move after the last candle done trimmed and burned.

> (**LUANNE, ABNER,** *and* **SARA** *look at each other, uneasy.* **SARA** *points the musket toward* **LUANNE.**)

SARA. You betta damn sho be kin by now. You betta damn sho not cross us.

9.

(Lights up on **MALIK** *in Sandra's office.* **CANDACE** *stands off to the side, writing Post-it notes and sticking them artistically across the dry-erase board. She practices active listening.)*

MALIK. You wanted to see me, Professor?

SANDRA. I have your paper.

MALIK. Is there a concern?

SANDRA. It's an excellent revision.

MALIK. It is?

SANDRA. Brilliant counterpoints. Your citing of the Black Codes to explain the economic powerlessness post-slavery juxtaposed with contemporary working people was illuminating, actually. I'd like to recommend your paper for publication in the student press.

MALIK. This...seriously?

SANDRA. Yes. Seriously.

MALIK. Wow. Thank you Professor.

SANDRA. Thank yourself. You took everything we discussed and you made significant changes that propelled the argument of your thesis. This is very good writing and you should be proud of yourself.

(She hands him back his paper.)

I give it an A+. Along with your other grade, this should balance you at an A- and the recommendation for publication should be a great boost to your scholarship review.

MALIK. I don't know what to say, Professor.

SANDRA. You don't need to say anything.

MALIK. But I feel sort of...bad.

SANDRA. It's okay to disagree with a professor, Malik. I'm not doing this because I want to be friends with you. I'm doing it because it's how I feel.

MALIK. Still, I just... I want to apologize though.

SANDRA. For what?

MALIK. I think I might've... I was just wrong, that's all. And I apologize.

SANDRA. Wrong about what?

MALIK. You. I thought you had... I'm just not sure anymore. But I think I misjudged you.

> (**CANDICE** *smirks.* **MALIK** *catches it. So does* **SANDRA.** *But they try to ignore it.*)

SANDRA. Okay. Well, hopefully you'll learn not to place judgment too soon on anyone. Makes for very limited vision.

MALIK. Yeah. I guess. Anyway, thanks.

> (**MALIK** *heads out, a little unsettled.*)

CANDICE. Totally insincere, right?

SANDRA. Candice, we don't need to discuss this.

CANDICE. I'm sorry Professor. I don't mean to be unprofessional as a student employee or whatever, but I just hate when dudes do that.

SANDRA. Do what exactly?

CANDICE. Just say I'm sorry for being a dick and yeah you're amazing and everything and I'm just gonna go back to having my male privilege and not really do anything about all the shit I put you through but uh, yeah, fuck you.

SANDRA. Might be projecting a bit.

CANDICE. It's totally a male chauvinism blindspot. Like why do they never have to be accountable for anything? Like fucking ever?

SANDRA. Candice is something wrong?

CANDICE. I need to tell you something.

(A tap on the office door. **SANDRA** *looks at* **CANDICE.** *Shit. Bad timing.)*

SANDRA. Come in!

(It's **JADE.***)*

JADE. Hey Sandra, I just wanted to drop by to say thank you.

SANDRA. You're welcome.

JADE. The letter you wrote on my behalf was really touching. I appreciate you honoring my work and vouching for my advancement to tenure.

SANDRA. Okay.

JADE. And about the other day...

SANDRA. Best to leave it there.

JADE. Right.

*(***JADE** *notices* **CANDICE.***)*

Did I interrupt your office hours?

SANDRA. Candice is my assistant. We were just talking work.

CANDICE. Hi Professor Banks.

JADE. Hi Candice. I'll let you two get back at it. Thank you again, Sandra. And Candice, remember you have an outstanding essay due in my inbox by five o'clock this afternoon. No excuses.

CANDICE. Yes ma'am.

(JADE *leaves.* CANDICE *fumes.*)

I totally hate her class.

SANDRA. You don't have to like every class. But you do have to do the work.

CANDICE. I swear she has it out extra good for me or something. Totally internalized woman hating. Way harder on me than the other students. I tried to pick up extra hours by assisting her, and I swear she gave it to Malik even though I asked first. But whatever. I don't have a right to complain even when it makes me itch. She's totally nothing like you.

SANDRA. And why would you think we'd be alike, exactly?

(CANDICE *stops talking and turns red.*)

CANDICE. Omigod. I was completely racist just then.

SANDRA. You're forgiven.

CANDICE. I didn't know it was so easy to… Just sort of creeps up on you.

SANDRA. It's unconscious bias. Checking it is what's important.

CANDICE. You're so forgiving.

SANDRA. I'm not that forgiving. Don't let it happen again.

CANDICE. I'm disgusted with myself. Malik was right.

SANDRA. Malik?

CANDICE. Um, nevermind.

SANDRA. Please don't feel the need to censor yourself now.

CANDICE. I talk too much. I'm really starting to see that now.

SANDRA. Candice, what are you talking about?

(Another knock at the door. It's **MALIK** *again.)*

Well this is a busy day.

MALIK. Professor, may I talk to you in private?

CANDICE. Malik, don't.

SANDRA. Is something wrong here?

MALIK. I have to. It's on my spirit.

CANDICE. Well fuck your spirit. You're completely inconsistent and insensitive and she doesn't need this right now.

MALIK. Candice, don't talk to me like that.

SANDRA. Excuse me. What is going on here?

CANDICE. Malik's about to unload a shitshow.

MALIK. I need to tell you about the image on your door.

CANDICE. Fucking stealing my thunder. I was going to tell her. I'm her assistant.

MALIK. You can tell whatever you want. But I'm sharing my peace.

SANDRA. What peace? Do you know who put the sign on my door?

MALIK. It wasn't intentional professor. I had no idea it would go viral.

SANDRA. What went viral?

*(**MALIK** hesitates. Looks at **CANDICE** for help.)*

CANDICE. Oh, NOW you want my help?

MALIK. It was in your inbox.

CANDICE. I didn't put it there!

MALIK. But you're the one who sent it to me.

CANDICE. But I didn't fucking put it there.

SANDRA. Who put what WHERE?

MALIK. I feel responsible because it was on my computer in Professor Banks' office. I opened it on a computer in her office.

CANDICE. I don't believe this. You're trying to throw me under the bus?

MALIK. I'm just being honest.

CANDICE. You couldn't be honest about who you're fucking, but now you can be honest?

MALIK. Don't do this here.

CANDICE. You're a slut.

MALIK. I'm non-committed. That doesn't make me a pig. Just cuz women say that shit doesn't make it true.

SANDRA. Stop this right now. Whatever personal behavior you two share, I don't want to hear another word of it. All I want to hear is how this image got on my door. NOW.

(They're silent for a moment.)

CANDICE. Malik.

MALIK. I didn't put the image on your door. I didn't do anything but...Photoshop your face. As a private joke. Not as something public. Not to humiliate or shame you. I regretted it immediately. I was on some angry shit about my grades –

CANDICE. It got sent to me by a classmate. Not the one with your face. Just the original photo. And I sent it to Malik because I thought it'd make him laugh.

SANDRA. What was the joke?

CANDICE. He was writing a paper on slavery and I was writing mine on white privilege. So I thought it'd be funny to give him an image of a white baby suckling a

Black slave woman...and the more I'm talking the more I'm seeing this was not funny.

SANDRA. As if to say...

MALIK. She's the white baby. Suckling the breast of her Black professor.

SANDRA. And that's me?

CANDICE. Professor Banks. Cuz I want to be nurtured by her – this is not good.

SANDRA. And how did it get to me?

MALIK. I responded with a Photoshop image of your face.

SANDRA. As if to say...

MALIK. That you coddle...

SANDRA. The white students.

CANDICE. Like me. Because it'd be an honor to suckle – nevermind.

> *(Pause. There is silence. Another knock at the door.)*

SANDRA. Yes?!

> *(JADE peeks in.)*

JADE. Oh. You're having a meeting.

SANDRA. Please, stay. It's just getting interesting.

JADE. Is everything okay?

SANDRA. Malik and Candice were just telling me about their inside joke that apparently went viral.

JADE. Oh.

MALIK. I didn't... I didn't make it go viral.

SANDRA. And how did it get on my door?

MALIK. I left it open by mistake. On my computer. In Professor Banks' office.

(They look at JADE.)

JADE. Wait a minute. I don't know what you all have been discussing, but I don't like how this is turning.

SANDRA. It wasn't you?

JADE. Are you kidding me? You're asking me this again? A fellow professor???

MALIK. I'm not saying Professor Banks.

CANDICE. She has a lot of assistants for different periods. Apparently still no room for me.

JADE. Sandra, I'm sorry that these two seem to have unleashed a can of worms, but I'm not sure this is traceable. Anyone could have come into my office. I have an open door.

SANDRA. It went viral?

MALIK. I got the email.

CANDICE. And me.

JADE. As did I. From a colleague. We were planning to address it ourselves with you at the faculty meeting. But then...

SANDRA. Someone printed it out and posted it on my door. Largely. For the entire department to see. And it could've been...anyone.

(They are all silent.)

I'm a target. A source of ridicule. Because I don't give you what you want when you want it, the way that makes you comfortable. Because I don't apologize for my stance on Black Lives Matter. Or bite my tongue when it comes to women or class. Everyone has permission to take shots and no one will be held accountable. No one will be held accountable. NO ONE.

(*A beat.*)

Get out of my office. GET THE MOTHERFUCK OUT!!!!!!!!!

(**SANDRA** *knocks things off of her desk in a rage. No one dares move.*)

(*After a moment, she looks around herself, finally free and simultaneously defeated.*)

(*Lights shift.*)

10.

(Lights up on **SARA**, *alone. She is dressed up better than we've ever seen her. She steps into a spotlight.)*

SARA. I'm a runaway. Name is Sara. They told me that I ought to tell you something 'bout me and slavery to help you be a friend for emancipation. So here I is.

(A picture is mounted, the one from the beginning of the play. It is in both women's worlds.)

This here be my mama. I carries it with me for protection. She done nursed white babies all her life and died a slave. I'm barren as a forest with no trees, and thought it made a curse of me as a woman. But it made me free. Bondage begin and end with me.

When that plantation went up in flames that fateful night of insurrection, I wasn't nowhere near it. Shame what happen with Master Dan gettin' stuck in his bedroom while his home was burnin'. Shame Missy Sue was pushed in there too. This be a war. Ain't no war without bloodshed. But I s'pect the ones who put folk in bondage already know that.

(Lights up on **SANDRA**, *alone in a separate world. The two women are parallel, and yet unaware of each other in these undefined spaces.* **SANDRA** *steps into the spotlight.)*

SANDRA. It has come to my attention that there will be no disciplinary action taken because of the uncontrollable source. That a non-harassment disclosure will be introduced at the top of the semester, which I'm supposed to receive as a victory. This is what it means to be at this institution. To know deep in your core that there will never be justice for you here.

SARA. This what it means to be in a peculiar institution. Under its boot, everybody yo' enemy. Even ones say they your friends. Long as there's a plantation, ain't none of us free.

SANDRA. This image was used to humiliate me. But I stand before you to say that I'm not ashamed.

SARA. I stand here before you to tell you that I am no more chattel and bond. I'm barren, but all woman, whole and full body.

(She bares her breast to the audience.)

Not to be nursin' your chir'ren or layin' in your bed. Not to be suckled from or auctioned off. Only to be governed by my own damn self.

SANDRA. I am no more your tolerant negro.

SARA. I am no more your slave nigger.

SANDRA & SARA. And that's all I have to say today. Thank you for your/yo' time.

(For the first time, SARA and SANDRA look at each other. Across generations and centuries of womanhood.)

(Lights fade on the women, seeing each other. Fully. Deeply. Seeing. Each. Other.)

End of Play